SIHA TOOSKIN KNOWS

The Strength of His Hair

By Charlene Bearhead and Wilson Bearhead

Illustrated by Chloe Bluebird Mustooch

HIGHWATER PRESS

Canada Council   Conseil des arts
for the Arts   du Canada

We acknowledge the support of the Canada Council for the Arts.
Nous remercions le Conseil des arts du Canada de son soutien.

HighWater Press gratefully acknowledges the financial support of the Province of Manitoba through the Department of Sport, Culture and Heritage and the Manitoba Book Publishing Tax Credit, and the Government of Canada through the Canada Book Fund (CBF), for our publishing activities.

HighWater Press is an imprint of Portage & Main Press.
Printed and bound in Canada by Friesens
Design by Relish New Brand Experience
Cover Art by Chloe Bluebird Mustooch

Library and Archives Canada Cataloguing in Publication

Title: Siha Tooskin knows the strength of his hair / by Charlene Bearhead and
    Wilson Bearhead ; illustrated by Chloe Bluebird Mustooch.
Other titles: Strength of his hair
Names: Bearhead, Charlene, 1963- author. | Bearhead, Wilson, 1958- author. |
    Mustooch, Chloe Bluebird, 1991- illustrator.
Identifiers: Canadiana (print) 20190058641 | Canadiana (ebook) 20190058676
    | ISBN 9781553798378 (softcover) | ISBN 9781553798392 (PDF) | ISBN
    9781553798385 (iPad fixed layout)
Classification: LCC PS8603.E245 S63 2020 | DDC jC813/.6—dc23

23 22 21 20   1 2 3 4 5

www.highwaterpress.com
Winnipeg, Manitoba
Treaty 1 Territory and homeland of the Métis Nation

I dedicate Siha Tooskin Knows the Strength of His Hair *to my oldest son, Storm, the inspiration for the character Siha Tooskin. Your strength and gifts are within you, gifted to you by the Creator. Embrace them and pass them on to your precious children.*

—CHARLENE BEARHEAD

We dedicate the Siha Tooskin Knows series to the storytellers who taught us. To those who guided us and shared their knowledge so that we might pass along what we have learned from them to teach children. Their stories are a gentle way of guiding us all along the journey of life.

In that way we tell these stories for our children and grandchildren, and for all children. May they guide you in the way that we have been guided as these stories become part of your story.

—CHARLENE BEARHEAD AND WILSON BEARHEAD

Watch for this little plant!
It will grow as you read, and if you need a break,
it marks a good spot for a rest.

Paul Wahasaypa's Mitoshin watched with amusement as his grandson carried firewood across the yard. Paul would carefully pick up one piece of wood at a time, inspect it to make sure it was fit for the woodpile, then carry each piece from the chopping block to the storage bin beside the house. As he arrived at the bin Paul would place each piece of wood with great care, as if he were creating a great work of art.

"Siha Tooskin," Mitoshin called out to his grandson with a gentle smile. "Why do you move so slowly? You didn't move that slowly when we were getting ready to go fishing yesterday."

Paul looked at Mitoshin but he didn't smile back. He only nodded his head to show that he had heard Mitoshin and then kept walking. He moved a little more quickly, but not exactly at the speed of light.

"We have to work faster today," said Mitoshin. "It's almost time to take you home." Paul knew that he had to get back home now that spring break was over. He had to start at his new school the next morning.

"Your mom will not be happy with me if I get you back too late for your first day of school," Mitoshin teased. "She might make me go in with you to explain to your teacher why you are so late. I am way too old to go back to school, Siha Tooskin."

Paul nodded. Once again, he did not smile. He just kept hauling the wood to the bin. "Aren't you happy to go home to see your mom and dad, Siha Tooskin?" Mitoshin asked, as he began to stack up wood in his own arms to help his grandson. "I thought you would be excited to start at your new school and to make new friends. That must be more exciting than carrying firewood around the yard with an old man."

"I liked my old school," answered Paul. "I wish my mom and dad didn't have to move to the new house. I know my mom wants a bigger house because a new baby is on the way," Paul said with an understanding tone. "I could have shared my room with the baby. That would be better than moving to a new school. I'd even share my room with Danny, even though he always gets into my stuff."

Then Paul turned to Mitoshin and his eyes brightened as though a light bulb had actually turned on inside his head. "Maybe I could just stay with you and Mugoshin."

Now Mitoshin knew something was wrong, because as much as Paul loved to visit he was always ready to go home to see his parents and little brother Danny again after a week or two.

Mitoshin placed his load of wood in the bin and sat down on a large section of white poplar nearby. "Pull up a stump, Siha Tooskin. You must be tired from all of those heavy loads of wood that you carried," he teased. He motioned to his grandson and pointed at another wood block on the ground beside him. Then Mitoshin's face changed and he took a more serious tone. "I would be happy to have you here with me, Mitowjin, but not if you are trying to hide from something at home."

"What is bothering you, Siha Tooskin? You know us old men can always talk to each other when something is heavy on our hearts or our minds," he coaxed with his knowing smile.

Paul sat with his head down for a minute as he considered Mitoshin's words. After a few minutes he raised his eyes and admitted, "I already met one of the boys on my new street before I came here, Mitoshin. When we were moving our stuff into the house the other day I saw a boy playing ball hockey in front of his garage. He was by himself shooting the ball into a net in his driveway, so when I rode my bike past his house I waved at him, then stopped to see if he wanted someone else to play ball hockey with. He looked like he was about my age and I thought maybe he would be in my class at my new school."

Then Paul looked down at the ground between his shoes. "The boy just made a face at me and said he didn't like girls. I told him I'm a boy and my name is Paul, so he would know that he could still play with me even if he only hangs out with boys. He just laughed at me and said I look like a girl with my braids."

Paul looked up sadly at his grandfather. "I don't want to go to school with people like that, Mitoshin."

Mitoshin nodded to show that he understood his grandson's feelings but he was not upset like Paul was. "Siha Tooskin..." Mitoshin was speaking in his usual gentle and caring tone. As strong as Mitoshin could be, Paul was always so grateful for the kindness that his voice carried whenever Paul needed it most. "You should pity this boy. You should not hide from him or hate him."

Paul was surprised at his grandfather's suggestion. "You think I should pity him when he made fun of me and hurt my feelings!"

"He does these things because he doesn't know any better, Siha Tooskin," Mitoshin explained. "This boy does not understand how to respect other people. You should pity him and even pray for him. Pray that the people who love him will learn more so that they can teach him to respect himself and others. That is what we have taught you to do, Siha Tooskin."

Paul looked down at an ant crawling on a piece of wood beside his foot. Though ants are so tiny, Ade had always taught Paul to respect them because they are such hard workers. Ade had also told him that the ants teach us the important lesson that it is not the size of our bodies but our ability to work together and stay focused on our tasks that makes us mighty.

Mitoshin counselled his grandson on the matter. "I know that you feel small like that ant sometimes, Siha Tooskin, but you have a huge heart. You have a strong spirit and a strong mind. You are bigger than the small minds and small words of people who have not been taught well." Paul reflected on what Mitoshin was saying and he knew Mitoshin was right.

Paul remembered how small he had been when his mom had first told him the story of why his hair was long. He thought about how his mom always took an extra-long time to gently comb out his hair when she was telling him stories to teach him the things that are important about life.

Ena had stories about humility and wisdom along with stories about bravery and kindness that Mugoshin and Mitoshin had passed along to her. She would tell him about teachings that came from the time before she was born and even before Mugoshin was born. Paul loved to hear

about those days when the grass grew very long and high upon the land.

One of the stories was actually about their hair and their braids. Ena talked about how the long, soft grass would blow in the wind and dance from side to side. The long, thick prairie grass gave Paul's people a soft place to rest when they set up their tipis and their camps. Ena told Paul how certain selected men would go ahead and find a good place to camp. They would weave and sway like the grass itself, as they trampled it

down beneath their moccasin-clad feet to make thick, soft mats on the ground where they would set up their homes and lodges. Ena explained that the people would grow their hair long like the prairie grass to remind them to be kind and gentle like the grass. She would tell Paul that his hair should remind him to be that way too.

"I know that I should be kind to the boy," Paul said as he looked up at Mitoshin. "But sometimes it's hard to do the right thing when someone hurts your feelings. I actually wanted to drop my bike and punch him, but then I remembered what Mom taught me about my hair reminding me to be kind."

Mitoshin smiled. He was proud of his grandson. "I know that these things can be hard when you feel alone and different from other children around you. But what does your mom say to you when she is braiding your hair?"

Paul responded without hesitation. "Ena tells me that we wear our hair in braids to remind us of our strength. Ena says that hitting someone isn't strength at all. She says that it takes real strength to stay true to our own ways. She says that the three strands of hair in a braid represent our body, mind, and spirit. She tells me I will grow up to be strong if I look after my body, mind, and spirit. It's important to keep them connected as one, like the hair in my braid." Paul grinned at Mitoshin. "I guess that is why my head hurts sometimes when my braids are really tight. Ena doesn't know her own strength."

Mitoshin laughed at the thought of his daughter pulling so hard to keep his grandson's braid tight and smooth. He was happy to see that Paul was getting his sense of humour back. He knew that Paul was feeling better about what he had to do when he went home.

"You see, you are very lucky, Siha Tooskin," Mitoshin explained to his grandson. "You have many relations who love you and teach you. We

treat you with respect so that you learn to respect
yourself and to respect all people. The braid that you
wear also reminds you of the strong bonds that hold
our family together. Now you see why you must pity
the boy you met. You can be thankful for the people
in our family and community who teach you to be
kind and strong and respectful. You need to try to
understand what this boy does not have and pray
for him so that he can learn respect and caring too."

"Okay, I will pray for him, Mitoshin," said Paul with some hesitation. "But what if he doesn't want to understand? What if he only laughs at me and tells the other boys at school to make fun of me and call me a girl?"

"Then you can laugh too, Siha Tooskin, because you know that this boy is even more pitiful than we thought. If they say you are weak like a girl or a woman, then they are really lost in their minds and spirits, because we know that women are the strength of our families and our Nation."

Mitoshin continued, "Our people have been through so many difficult times. We have withstood so much over the years. Even the environment and the weather can make life hard. All of the offenses against our people by colonizers...so many challenging times. Laughter is one of the things that has helped us to get through those difficult times. Our teachings, our spirituality, and our humour are some of our greatest strengths. Our mothers and grandmothers teach us these

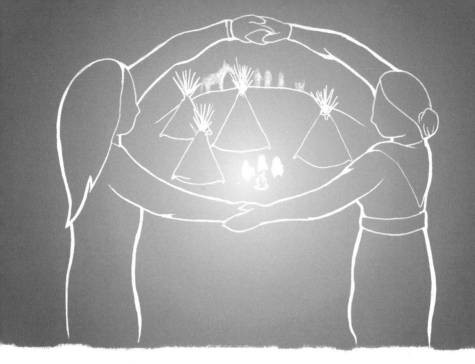

lessons from a young age and they hold our families together. You can laugh because you know that the thing they are teasing you about is the thing that reminds you to be strong."

Mitoshin gave his grandson a playful look. "Besides, if this boy wants to see something really funny he should see you before your hair is brushed and braided. I've seen that messy head when you wake up in the morning. Now that's funny!"

Paul chuckled. "I guess you're right. He'd probably really crack up if he saw that. I even make myself laugh some mornings when I look in the mirror."

Mitoshin stood up and walked back over to the chopping block. He loaded up an armful of firewood and started to carry it over to the bin. "Yes, Siha Tooskin," Mitoshin teased, "The boy would find that funny. He would laugh even harder if he saw you running down the road chasing my truck. That's what will happen if you don't finish this woodpile on time because I'll have to leave you behind."

"Yeah," said Paul as he loaded up his arms with six pieces of wood at one time. "We'd better hurry. I have to get home so I can be ready to start at my new school tomorrow. There might be lots of things the other kids and I can learn from each other there after all."

Glossary

Ade	Dad or father
Ena	Mom or mother
Mitoshin	Grandfather
Mitowjin	My grandchild
Mugoshin	Grandmother
Siha Tooskin	Little Foot (siha is foot; tooskin is little)
Wahasaypa	Bear head

A note on use of the Nakota language in this book series from Wilson Bearhead:

The Nakota dialect used in this series is the Nakota language as taught to Wilson by his grandmother, Annie Bearhead, and used in Wabamun Lake First Nation. Wilson and Charlene have chosen to spell the Nakota words in this series phonetically as Nakota was never a written language. Any form of written Nakota language that currently exists has been developed in conjunction with linguists who use a Eurocentric construct.

ABOUT THE AUTHORS

Charlene Bearhead is an educator and Indigenous education advocate. She was the first Education Lead for the National Centre for Truth and Reconciliation and the Education Coordinator for the National Inquiry into Missing and Murdered Indigenous Women and Girls. Charlene was recently honoured with the Alumni Award from the University of Alberta and currently serves as the Director of Reconciliation for *Canadian Geographic*. She is a mother and a grandmother who began writing stories to teach her own children as she raised them. Charlene lives near Edmonton, Alberta with her husband Wilson.

Wilson Bearhead, a Nakota Elder and Wabamun Lake First Nation community member in central Alberta (Treaty 6 territory), is the recent recipient of the Canadian Teachers' Federation Indigenous Elder Award. Currently, he is the Elder for Elk Island Public Schools. Wilson's grandmother Annie was a powerful, positive influence in his young life, teaching him all of the lessons that gave him the strength, knowledge, and skills to overcome difficult times and embrace the gifts of life.

ABOUT THE ILLUSTRATOR

Chloe Bluebird Mustooch is from the Alexis Nakoda Sioux Nation of central Alberta, and is a recent graduate of the Emily Carr University of Art + Design. She is a seamstress, beadworker, illustrator, painter, and sculptor. She was raised on the reservation, and was immersed in hunting, gathering, and traditional rituals, and she has also lived in Santa Fe, New Mexico, an area rich in art and urbanity.